The BOOKSTORE CAT

BY
CYLIN BUSBY

ILLUSTRATED BY
CHARLES SANTOSO

BALZER + BRAY
An Imprint of HarperCollins *Publishers*

The Bookstore Cat is inspired by a Victorian parlor game that I played with my family when I was a child, The Minister's Cat. In that game, a cat is described using adjectives in alphabetical order. Players sit in a circle and establish a clapping rhythm. The first player describes the minister's cat with an adjective that begins with the letter *A*, and the next player will do the same using the letter *B*. ("The minister's cat is an angry cat." "The minister's cat is a bossy cat." And so on . . .) If a player cannot think of an adjective, they are "out," and the next player must assume that letter and quickly think of an adjective. If a player cannot keep the rhythm or clapping pattern, they are also declared "out."

Popular in England (and New England) since the mid-1800s, the game is still played around the holidays.

—C.B.

Balzer + Bray is an imprint of HarperCollins Publishers.
The Bookstore Cat Text copyright © 2020 by Cylin Busby Illustrations copyright © 2020 by Charles Santoso All rights reserved. Manufactured in Italy.
No part of this book may be used or reproduced in any manner whatsoever without written permission except in the case of brief quotations embodied in critical articles and reviews.
For information address HarperCollins Children's Books, a division of HarperCollins Publishers, 195 Broadway, New York, NY 10007. www.harpercollinschildrens.com

Library of Congress Control Number: 2019951909
ISBN 978-0-06-289434-2

The artist used Adobe Photoshop to create the digital illustrations for this book. Typography by Dana Fritts 20 21 22 23 24 RTLO 10 9 8 7 6 5 4 3 2 1 ❖ First Edition

The bookstore cat is an **a**dorable cat.

The bookstore cat is a **b**ossy

(very bossy)

but **C**uddly cat.

The bookstore cat is a **d**arting cat,

an excited cat,

a **f**riendly cat.

The bookstore cat is a **g**orgeous cat,

though, of course, he's also a **h**umble cat,

an **I**ntelligent cat,

and a **j**ealous cat.

Sometimes he acts like a **k**ittenish cat.

But he is always a loyal cat.

The bookstore cat is a **m**ysterious cat,

when he's not a **n**aughty cat.

He knows how to be an **O**bedient cat

or a very, very **p**atient cat.

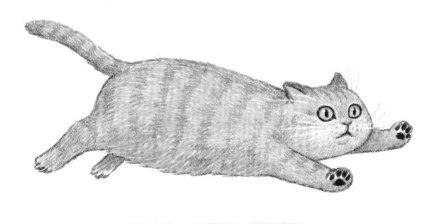

The bookstore cat is a **q**uick cat

and a **r**egal cat.

And a **S**leepy . . . oh-so-sleepy cat . . .

After a nap, he's a **t**hirsty cat.

Uh-oh! The bookstore cat is an **U**nderwater cat!

And a **V**ocal cat!

The bookstore cat is a **W**aiting . . .

waiting . . .

w a i t i n g cat.

Pounce!
He's a **X**enops-chasing cat.

The bookstore cat is a ucky cat. Ew!

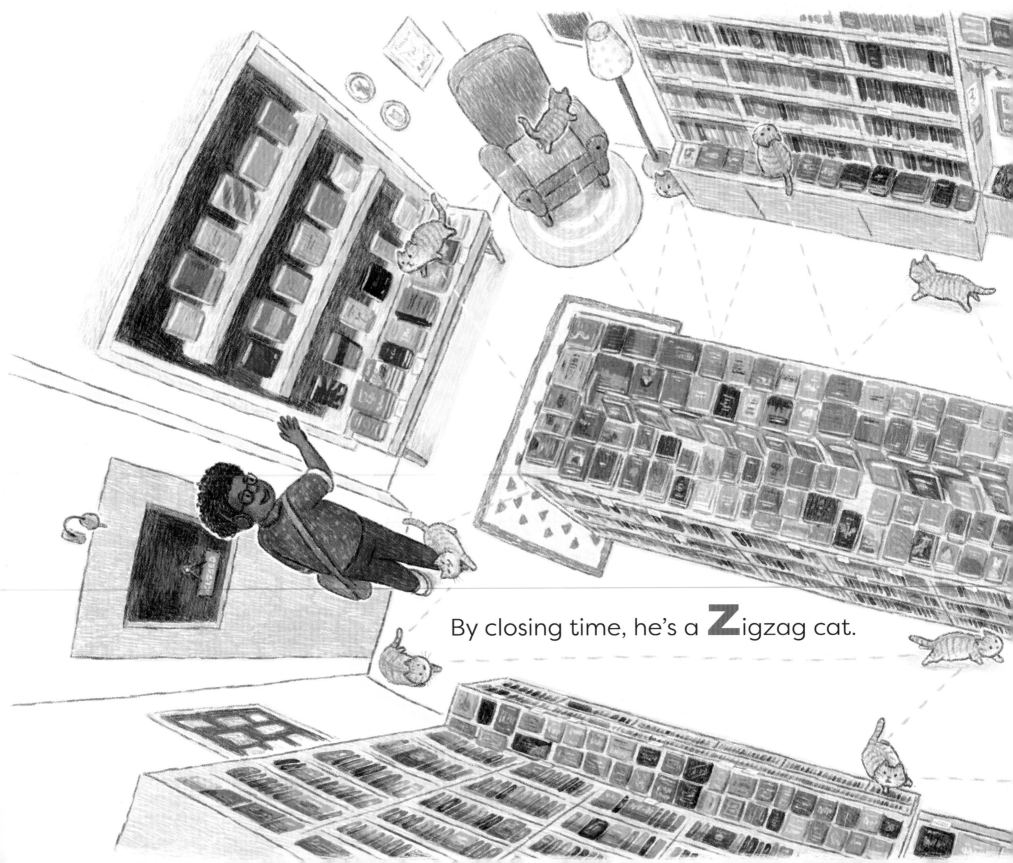

By closing time, he's a **Z**igzag cat.

The bookstore cat is all of these, from A to Z,
but, most important of all, he is . . .
the bookstore cat.